Stop the Presses!

By Steven Banks
Illustrated by Vince DePorter

SpongeBob ran out of his house. "Patrick!" he called out. "We're going to do the greatest thing we have ever done!"

"Are we going to look at my rock?" asked Patrick.

"No," said SpongeBob. "We're going to start our very own newspaper!"

"What's a newspaper?" Patrick asked.

"It's a piece of paper with information and stories and events," SpongeBob explained. "We'll write the articles and take pictures."

"Okay, but I get to name it," said Patrick. "How about 'News Made Up by SpongeBob and Patrick'!"

"Here's a camera," said SpongeBob. "Go all over Bikini Bottom and take pictures of amazing things."

"Gotcha!" said Patrick. "What are *you* going to do?"

SpongeBob smiled. "I'm going to interview one of the most fascinating subjects in town!"

SpongeBob interviewed his pet snail, Gary.
"Now, Gary, may I call you 'Gary'?" asked SpongeBob.
"Meow," said Gary.
"Thanks!" said SpongeBob. "Do you enjoy living with the delightful SpongeBob SquarePants?"
"Meow," said Gary.

SpongeBob giggled. "I knew it! Now, tell me, is he the best fry cook you know?"

"Meow," said Gary.

"Wow, thanks again! Okay, last question. Do you love him as much as he loves you?" asked SpongeBob.

"Meow," said Gary.

Patrick ran off to take pictures. Suddenly he saw his rock.
"Wow! Look at this amazing rock!" he cried. "I've got to take a picture of this! I've never seen anything like it! Say 'cheese,' please!"

The next morning SpongeBob and Patrick stood on a corner in downtown Bikini Bottom holding out copies of their newspaper.

"Extra! Extra! Read all about it!" shouted SpongeBob. "Gary comes clean in shocking interview!"

Patrick yelled, "And in the same issue, the amazing rock!"

But no one bought a newspaper. Everyone just walked by.
"Why won't anyone buy our newspaper?" SpongeBob wondered aloud.
"They must be rock haters!" said Patrick.

"Hey, Squidward!" said SpongeBob. "I bet you came here to buy a copy of our brand-new newspaper!"

"No," said Squidward. "I came here to laugh at you two nincompoops! You'd have to pay *me* to read that stupid newspaper!"

"Okay, here's a dollar," said SpongeBob. "Read it and tell us why people aren't buying it."

"Look, this is boring," said Squidward. "Who wants to read about a snail or look at a picture of a rock?"

"But it's an amazing rock!" said Patrick.

Squidward shook his head. "People want to read juicy gossip and see embarrassing photos."

"Of rocks?" asked Patrick.

"STOP TALKING ABOUT ROCKS!" yelled Squidward.

Patrick whispered to SpongeBob, "He must be a rock hater too."

"Squidward is right," said SpongeBob. "We've got to get the dirt on everyone!"

"Okay, here's my shovel," said Patrick.

"No, not that kind of dirt, Patrick," said SpongeBob. "We have to find out everyone's deep, dark secrets."

Later that night SpongeBob and Patrick went to Mr. Krabs's house and peeked in the window.

Mr. Krabs was putting dollar bills in little beds and kissing them good night! "Sleep tight, my little loves!"

The next day they spied on Sandy Cheeks. She was hanging her clothes on the clothesline.

They spied on Plankton, who was singing a love song to his computer wife, Karen.

Plankton sang in his deep voice:

"Karen, my love, you are more beautiful than the freeways in Cincinnati! I love you almost as much as I would love to get the secret recipe to make a Krabby Patty!"

They even snuck into Squidward's bathroom and spied on him taking a bath *and* playing his clarinet!

The next day SpongeBob and Patrick were out selling their newspaper. "Plankton sings corny love songs! Sandy Cheeks hangs clothes out to dry! Mr. Krabs kisses his money! Squidward takes baths with a clarinet!" they shouted.

Bikini Bottom Gazette

SANDY HANGS 'EM UP!

KRABS'S SECRET LOVE

MUSICAL SQUID ALL WET

PLANKTON SINGS!

"Why are y'all sneaking around taking pictures of me?" Sandy demanded.

"I only kiss me money on Tuesday nights!" cried Mr. Krabs.

"My songs aren't corny," Plankton said, complaining. "They are masterpieces of love!"

"This is an invasion of privacy," said Squidward. "And you didn't even get my good side!"

"If you can't print something nice, don't print anything at all," said Sandy. Mr. Krabs nodded. "Aye, the lass is right. It was a mean thing to do, lads!"

"I'm sorry," cried SpongeBob. "We didn't mean to hurt anybody, we just wanted to sell our newspaper! We won't do it anymore!"

"We should have stuck with rocks," Patrick said, sobbing.

"We're getting out of the newspaper business, Patrick," said SpongeBob. "But what are we going to do with all these newspapers?" Patrick asked. SpongeBob snapped his fingers. "Don't worry. I've got a great idea!"

"Paper hats here!" shouted SpongeBob. "Come get your paper hats!"
"Hats for sale!" yelled Patrick. "Perfect for wearing while looking at rocks!"
SpongeBob laughed. "Patrick, I think this is the beginning of a very successful business!"